Poodlena

To my dog, Max, and my sister, Victoria

Copyright © 2004 by E. B. McHenry
First published by Bloomsbury Publishing 2004
This edition published 2005

Typeset in Mona Lisa
Art created with gouache

Published by Bloomsbury Publishing, New York, London, and Berlin
Distributed to the trade by Holtzbrinck Publishers

Library of Congress Cataloging-in-Publication Data
McHenry, E. B.
Poodlena / by E. B. McHenry
p. cm.
Summary: Poodlena Pompadour, a perfectly groomed pink poodle, discovers the joys of playing in a muddy dog park.
ISBN-10: 1-58234-824-3 • ISBN-13: 978-1-58234-824-7 (hardcover)
ISBN-10: 1-58234-698-4 • ISBN-13: 978-1-58234-698-4 (paperback)
[1. Poodles—Fiction. 2. Dogs—Fiction. 3. Grooming—Fiction. 4. Behavior—Fiction. 5. Stories in rhyme.] I. Title.
PZ8.M1597 Po 2003   [E]—dc21   2002028347

Printed in China
1 3 5 7 9 10 8 6 4 2

Bloomsbury Publishing, Children's Books, U.S.A.
175 Fifth Avenue, New York, NY 10010

Poodlena

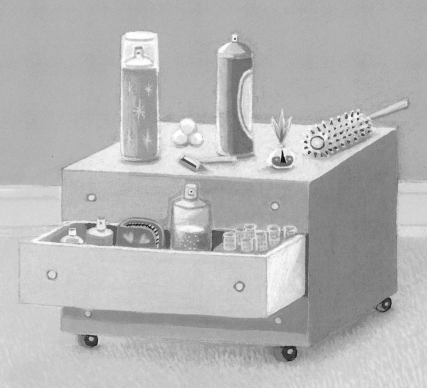

by E. B. McHenry

BLOOMSBURY
CHILDREN'S
BOOKS

In a big-city high-rise
On the very top floor
Lived a pink, fluffy poodle—
Poodlena Pompadour.

She wore on her head
A pink mountain of hair,
As light as a feather
And mostly pink air.

Days were spent teasing her fabulous fluff—
Shaving legs, painting toenails, and other such stuff.

It took lots of work and a good bit of spray
To look pretty and perfect in just the right way.

She'd fuss and she'd tweeze,

She'd paint and she'd fluff,

She'd powder, perfume,

And pink herself up.

When finally finished,
Leashed, late in the day,
She'd leave for the park
For the dog time to play.

Down, down she'd go
At three quarters past four
To the elegant lobby
From the very top floor.

From the elegant lobby, out revolving glass doors,
Through rush-hour traffic, past big-city stores.

At five she'd arrive
To a wild dog park scene

Where dogs whizzed around
Fetching balls on the green.

But she kept far away
From their
    ball-fetching jaws,
Away from wet noses
And mud-padded paws

Safe on the sidewalk,
All fluffed, pink, and clean,
Never running or sniffing,
Wanting just to be seen.

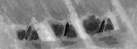

One night storm clouds blew in.
Heavy rains filled the sky.
No dog park for days—
She stayed in, clean and dry.

She fussed and she tweezed,

She painted and fluffed,

She powdered, perfumed,

And pinked herself up.

When the rain finally stopped,
She returned to the scene
And arrived extra pink,
Extra fluffed up and clean.

But disaster had struck—
The park was afloat.
Mud covered the sidewalk—
It looked like a moat.

The mud was a river, an ocean, a sea.
She felt kind of itchy; did she feel a flea?

She did feel a flea—in fact she felt three.
Stopping to scratch, she was hit!
Suddenly. . .

She flew up in the air,
Spinning round and around,
Getting covered in mud
As she slid to the ground.

Her mountain of hair
Hung soggy and small,
Her pink, perfect look
Somehow lost in the fall.

Woozy but wagging,
Shaken up but not down,
She was chased by a chow—
So she chased him around!

She raced after balls—
Fetching more than a few,
Staying late, playing games
Till all vanished from view.

With so many balls
To be fetched in a day,
Now she fluffs a bit less
And makes more time to play.

One powder with pink
And then off to the park...

To chase balls on the green
And get dirty till dark.